will you be my friend?

Russell Ayto

Andersen Press USA

"I'm lonely.
I have **no friends**,"
says Bush Baby.

"Will you be my friend?"

"No way," says Giraffe.
"You're much **too** small.
I can hardly see you
down there."

"Will you be my friend?"

"Nah. You have a **tail**," says Toad.
"I don't understand tails. Mine vanished when I was a tadpole. You should have a l-o-n-g tongue instead."

"Will you be my friend?"

"What?" says Zebra.
"I can't be seen with you.

You have **no stripes**.
Where are your stripes?
No stripes won't do."

"Will you be my friend?"

"Don't be ss-silly,"
says Snake.
"You have far **too**
many legs-ss.

See? No legs-ss."

"Will . . ."

"Absolutely not," says Flamingo.
"Don't even think about it.
You're totally the wrong color.
PINK is the right color.
P.I.N.K. PINK!"

"No one wants to be **my** friend.
Nobody even likes me.
Nobody in the whole wide world.
I'll just go away and be on my own . . .
forever."

"I can't decide,"
says Lion.
"Are you very brave,
or very foolish?"

"I'm **very** lonely," says Bush Baby. "I have no friends. And nobody wants to be my friend."

"Oh," says Lion.
"I have no friends either.
Everyone thinks
I might eat them for
some reason.

But I would **never** eat a friend.
That would be **most** unfriendly."

"Will you be . . .
oh I know,
I look all **wrong**
to be your friend."

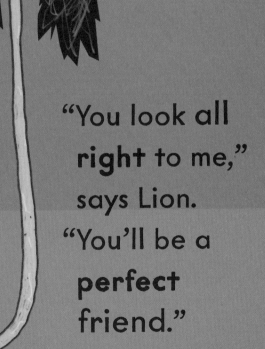

"You look all **right** to me," says Lion. "You'll be a **perfect** friend."

Then all the other animals say,
"We'd like to be **your** friends **now**."

Bush Baby says,
"What do you think,
Lion?"

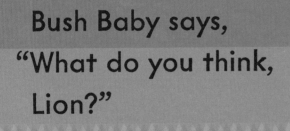

And Lion says,
"I think I'm getting **very** . . ."

HUNG